GREASY GRIMY
GOPHER GUTS

CAMP RUN-A-MUCK

GREASY GRIMY GOPHER GUTS

TODD STRASSER

AN
APPLE
PAPERBACK

SCHOLASTIC INC.
New York Toronto London Auckland Sydney

To those wild and crazy campers, Sam and Charlie
Roberts. And to Lily, the adorable camper-to-be.

ISBN 0-590-74261-2

10 9 8 7 6 5 4 3 2   7 8 9/9 0 1 2/0

Printed in the U.S.A.   40
First Scholastic printing, June 1997

CHAPTER

"Hey, Lucas, what did the Abominable Snowman have for breakfast?" my friend Justin asked.

"Huh?" He'd caught me dozing. We were sitting together on a bus, going upstate.

"I said, what did the Abominable Snowman have for breakfast?" Justin repeated.

"I don't know. What?"

"Frosted Flakes!" Justin grinned. "Frosted . . . Snowman. Get it?"

I nodded. "Sure, Justin, I get it."

He frowned. "Then how come you're not laughing?"

"I guess I'm just wondering about this job at Camp Run-a-Muck you talked me into," I said. "What kind of name is Run-a-Muck?"

"Must be some Native American thing," he said. "Don't worry about it."

I gazed out the bus window. We were on a highway

passing a farm with a big red barn. Black and white cows were grazing in the fields.

"Hey, Lucas," Justin said. "Did you hear about the shipload of cows that disappeared?"

"No," I said.

"They were last seen in the Ber-moo-da Triangle," he said. "Get it?"

I groaned. Justin's jokes were awful.

"What if they find out we lied about our ages?" I asked.

Justin shook his head. He's average height, like me, with straight brown hair parted in the middle. "No way. We're not going to get caught."

"The job form said the minimum age is sixteen," I said. "I'm fourteen, and you're thirteen. You don't think *someone* will notice that we look kind of young?"

"Not if we act real mature," said Justin. "That reminds me. Did you hear about the eight-year-old kid who climbed Mount Everest?"

I shook my head.

"He wanted to peak at an early age!" Justin grinned. "Peak, like mountain peak! Get it?"

"Sure, Justin, I get it. That's real mature?"

"Hey, come on, Lucas, lighten up." He poked me with his elbow. "You're as strong as any sixteen-year-old. You're a good athlete, and everyone likes you. You have nothing to worry about."

"Except for one thing," I said.

"What?" asked Justin.

"We're supposed to work in the Camp Run-a-Muck kitchen," I said. "We've been hired as assistant cooks."

"Right," said Justin. "So what's the problem?"

"Neither of us knows how to cook," I said.

CHAPTER

2

The bus turned down a narrow road lined on both sides by tall pines. Suddenly there were no more farms or fields, just thick green trees.

"Not knowing how to cook is not a problem," Justin said. "We're talking about a camp, not some fancy restaurant. You ever been to camp, Lucas?"

"Nope," I said.

"I have news for you," Justin said. "You can feed those kids just about anything as long as it doesn't crawl off the plate."

I turned and looked at him. "*You* ever been to camp, Justin?"

He shook his head.

"Then how do you know what we can feed them?" I asked.

"My cousin Joey told me," Justin said. "He went to a camp where the food was so bad, the kids almost starved to death."

The bus stopped at a restaurant made out of logs. Out in front people were eating at picnic tables. A big red and white sign on top of the restaurant said LOG CABIN PIZZA.

"All right!" Justin rubbed his hands together. "Must be lunchtime!"

The bus driver said we had twenty minutes to eat. Justin and I got off the bus and stretched our legs.

"Finally, we're in the country!" Justin took a deep breath of country air, then he frowned. "Wait a minute! It smells like the stuff my mother sprays in the bathroom!"

"That's the smell of pine trees," I said.

"Gee," Justin muttered. "I can't believe I came all the way to the country and it smells like my bathroom."

"You've got it mixed up," I said. "The country doesn't smell like your bathroom. Your bathroom smells like the country."

"Same difference." Justin shrugged. "But that reminds me of a joke."

I wasn't surprised. *Everything* reminded Justin of a joke.

"You hear about the guy who moved to the city?" he asked.

"Nope," I said.

"He heard the country was at war," Justin said

with a grin. "The country was at war, so he moves to the city. Get it?"

"Sure, Justin," I said with a groan.

Justin put his hands on his hips. "Aren't you *ever* going to laugh at one of my jokes?"

"Yes," I said. "When you tell me one that's *funny*."

Justin sighed. "Let's go get some pizza."

We sat down at one of the picnic tables and ordered slices of pizza from a waitress. While we waited, we listened to birds chirping in the trees. Then a gray animal about the size of a cat crawled out of the woods and started gnawing on some grass.

"What's that?" Justin asked.

"A gopher," I said.

"Cute little guy, huh?" Justin grinned. "Man, I just know this is going to be a *great* summer experience. We'll make some money. And on our days off we can hang around the lake, swim, get a tan, meet girls, play some ball. Believe me, you never saw such a great time."

"And I never saw *that*, either," I replied, pointing down the road.

CHAPTER 3

A strange-looking guy was walking along the road toward us. He had a bushy gray beard and long scraggly gray hair, and was dressed in ragged clothes. He was wearing a headband and beads, and sort of looked like a hippie from the 1960s. In one hand he carried a stick. With the other hand he dragged a dirty brown burlap bag along the ground.

He stopped in the middle of the road and started to poke something on the ground with his stick.

"What's he doing?" Justin asked.

The hippie guy slowly bent down and picked up the thing he'd been poking. It was gray, furry, and flat.

"Looks like he just picked up a squashed squirrel," I said.

The hippie guy brought the squashed squirrel to his nose and sniffed it. Then he opened his burlap sack and dropped in the crushed critter.

"Oh, gross!" Justin gasped. "He *collects* dead animals."

The hippie guy came toward us, then stopped again. This time he picked up something flat and round. It was a dark color and had some short, stubby things poking out of it.

"Now what's he got?" Justin asked.

"Looks like a turtle," I said, watching the hippie guy put it in his sack.

An awful, burning stench engulfed us. "Gross!" Justin cried. "What's that smell?"

"I think it's coming from him," I gasped, wiping the tears from my eyes. The odor was so strong it burned. "It's a dead-animal-body-odor combo!"

Pinching their noses closed, the people at the other tables began to leave. Just then the waitress came out of the restaurant.

"Here you go, boys." She put our slices on the table.

Justin pointed at the hippie guy. "What's with him?"

"Oh, no." The waitress groaned, then shouted, "Get out of here, Roadkill Man. You're scaring away the customers."

Roadkill Man nodded and turned away, taking the stench with him.

"Is he like a hermit?" I asked the waitress.

"Yes," she said. "He's been around here forever."

"Way weird," Justin said. "What does he do with those squashed animals?"

"Eats 'em, I guess." The waitress left to take someone else's order.

Justin and I stared at each other in disbelief.

"He *eats* that stuff?" I repeated, totally grossed out.

"Lost your appetite?" Justin asked.

I nodded.

Justin pointed at my plate. "Then could I have your slice?"

"Are you serious?" I asked as my friend took a bite of my pizza.

"Hey, everyone has to eat," Justin said.

CHAPTER

4

Back on the bus a little while later, Justin picked his teeth with a toothpick. "You think he has recipes?"

"Who?" I said.

"Roadkill Man. You think he has recipes for the squashed animals he finds?"

I looked at him like he was crazy. "What are you talking about?"

"Know how your mom makes macaroni and cheese?" Justin said. "Maybe Roadkill Man makes squashed squirrel and fleas. Or how about Shake 'n Bake snake?"

"Did anyone ever tell you that you're totally sick?" I asked.

We weren't on the bus for long when it stopped on the side of the road again.

"Anyone going to Camp Run-a-Muck, this is your stop," the driver said.

"That's us," Justin said, getting up.

The driver got off the bus and opened the luggage compartment so we could get our backpacks.

"You boys working at the camp this summer?" he asked.

"That's right," Justin said.

The driver narrowed his eyes and squinted at us. "Aren't you both a little *young*?"

"Oh, no, sir," Justin said. "We're both sixteen."

The driver smiled. "Well, when you can't take it anymore, I come through here every day at two P.M."

"When we can't take *what* anymore?" Justin asked.

"You'll find out soon enough," the bus driver said, and climbed back on the bus. The engine rumbled, and the bus pulled back onto the road, leaving us in a cloud of exhaust and dust.

CHAPTER

5

"**W**hat do you think he meant by that?" Justin asked.

"I don't know," I said. I was looking across the road at an old hand-painted sign that said Camp Run-a-Muck.

We walked past the sign and started to follow a trail through the woods. The air was cool and the trail was shaded by the tall pine trees. Justin stopped near a tree with pink and white flowers blooming from its branches. "Hey, Lucas, I think this is a dogwood."

"How do you know?" I asked.

"I can tell by the bark," Justin said. "*Dog-*wood . . . bark. Get it?"

"What I don't get is how you can make jokes at a time like this," I said.

"Why not?" Justin asked.

"Didn't you hear the bus driver?" I said. "No one can stand working at this camp."

"What does he know?" Justin said. "He doesn't work there."

We followed the trail up a hill. At the top was an old wooden forest-rangers' tower. A ladder went up the side of the tower. I put down my backpack and started to climb.

"Where're you going?" Justin asked.

"I want to see what's around," I said.

I climbed to the top of the tower. Justin followed me up. He was a little out of breath.

"Hear about the guy who dropped a clock from the top of a ladder?" he asked.

"No."

"He wanted to see time fly."

"Yuck, yuck," I said, and looked around. It was a clear day, and you could see in all directions. Mostly you saw the green tops of pine trees. But down the other side of the hill was a vast grassy clearing beside a wide blue lake. In part of the clearing was a ball field; some tennis courts; a couple of large, low buildings; and a bunch of smaller cabins. The other part was a broad green golf course with white sand traps and red flags at each hole.

"Guess that's Camp Run-a-Muck," Justin said. "I don't remember reading anything about there being golf."

"Neither do I," I said.

"That's weird," said Justin. "Here we are in the middle of the woods, a million miles from anywhere. How many people could want to play golf?"

"You got me," I said with a shrug. I was just about to climb back down when I noticed a gray satellite dish attached to the tower.

"What do you think that's doing here?" I asked.

Justin shrugged. "Maybe the bears watch ESPN."

CHAPTER

6

Back on the ground we picked up our backpacks and continued along the trail.

"Why did the turkey cross the road?" Justin asked.

"I don't know."

"To prove he wasn't chicken."

We left the woods and entered the camp. There were a few people around. Someone was painting the flagpole. Someone else was cutting the grass. It looked like they were preparing the camp for its official opening the next day.

"Where do we go?" I asked.

"Let's try in here." Justin pointed at a long, wide, green building.

Inside were rows of tables. Down at one end was a stage. Colorful banners hung along the walls, and the air smelled like sour milk.

"Smells like we're in the dining hall," I said.

"Hey, look." Justin pointed toward a small room

near the doors. A girl with long blond hair was working behind a counter. Racks of candy lined the walls, along with pictures of ice-cream bars.

"Maybe she knows where we should go," Justin said.

We went over to the counter. The blond girl looked up and smiled at us. She had even, white teeth, bright blue eyes, and a turned-up nose. In other words, she was beautiful.

"Hi, guys," she said.

I waited for Justin to say something, but he just stared at her with his mouth hanging open.

"Hi," I said. "I'm Lucas Harmon, and this is Justin Cushing. We're working here this summer."

"Nice to meet you," she said. "I'm Amanda Kirby. I'll be running the canteen."

"I thought a canteen was something you put water in," I said.

"It also means a little candy store like this," Amanda said.

"What do you call a book that a skunk would read?" Justin suddenly asked.

"A best-*smeller*?" Amanda guessed.

Justin looked surprised. "Hey! You're good!"

Amanda smiled shyly. "Thanks. So where are you guys going to work?"

"The kitchen," Justin said. "We're assistant cooks."

"Then you've come to the right place," Amanda said. "The kitchen's in there." She pointed at

16

two brown swinging doors about fifty feet away.

"Come on," I said to Justin. "Let's go check it out."

"Just a second," Justin said, turning to Amanda. "Why did the idiot cut a hole in his umbrella?"

"Hmmm. That's a hard one." Amanda rested her chin on her hand and thought. "I know! He wanted to see if it had stopped raining?"

"Amazing!" Justin gasped in wonder.

"Let's go to the kitchen," I said, leading him away.

We were walking toward the kitchen when the doors suddenly swung open in front of us. Out stepped a big fat man wearing brown and white golf shoes, red and green plaid pants, and a yellow polo shirt. Little trails of sweat ran down his forehead and around his beady little eyes. His arms were as thick as tree trunks, and his belly jiggled like Jell-O under the yellow polo shirt.

Behind him staggered a skinny guy with curly brown hair. He was bent over by the weight of a heavy black golf bag filled with clubs.

The big fat man glowered at us. "What are *you* doing here?"

17

CHAPTER

7

"Camp doesn't open until tomorrow," the fat man grumbled.

"We got a letter that said we were supposed to get here a day early," Justin stammered.

"Letter?" the fat man scowled. "What letter? I didn't send you campers a letter."

"We're not campers," I said. "We're assistant cooks."

The fat man's beady eyes widened for a second. "That's different. I'm Bob Kirby, and I own this camp. What're your names?"

"Lucas Harmon," I said.

"Justin Cushing," said Justin.

Kirby reached into his pocket and pulled out a small packet of ketchup. He ripped it open with his teeth and started to suck on it.

"How old are you, Cushing?" he asked.

Justin swallowed nervously. "Uh, sixteen."

"Yeah, right. And I'm Spiderman." Kirby smirked. "Either of you kids know how to cook?"

Justin and I nodded slowly.

"Bull," Kirby said. "I'll bet you don't even know how to crack an egg."

Then he told us to go find a place called "the bunkhouse," where we were going to live for the summer.

"It's two-thirty now," Kirby said. "At three o'clock we'll meet in the kitchen. Got that?"

"Got it," said Justin. We started away.

"Wait a minute!" Kirby growled.

Justin and I stopped and turned.

"Either of you have any serious diseases?" Kirby asked. "Hepatitis? Tuberculosis? Plague?"

Justin and I shook our heads.

"Good," Kirby said. "Now get going."

CHAPTER

8

"**G**uess we just met the owner of the camp," I said as we went outside to find the bunkhouse.

"Bob 'The Blob' was a slob," muttered Justin. "Sucked on ketchup and barfed a gob."

The bunkhouse was a long, narrow building. Justin and I went in.

The air was hot and musty inside. A dozen double-decker bunks lined the walls. The floorboards creaked, and the place smelled old. Initials were carved into the walls and rafters.

Justin was humming to himself:

"Great green gobs of greasy grimy gopher guts
Mutilated monkey meat
Chopped-up birdy's feet.
French-fried eyeballs rolling up and down the
  street
Oops! I forgot my spoon!"

"What's that?" I asked.

"Old camp song," he said.

"I thought you've never been to camp," I said.

"My cousin Joey taught me," he said. "Hey, what's that?"

Hanging from the rafters were long yellow strips of tape with brown spots on them.

"Haven't you ever seen flypaper before?" a voice asked.

Justin and I looked around. Sitting on one of the bunks was a tall black guy.

"They make it real sticky and put a scent on it that flies love," the guy said. "A fly lands on it and gets stuck. Then it starts to die a slow, miserable death from starvation. You know what happens in starvation?"

Justin and I shook our heads.

"The body can't get food, so it starts to feed on itself," the guy said. "Like self-cannibalization. First it eats its own fat. Then it eats its own muscles. Then the internal organs. The liver, kidneys, and heart . . . it just eats itself alive. The heart walls get thinner and thinner until *boom*! It explodes. After that there's nothing left except a puddle of bones and blood inside a loose bag of skin."

"Who are you?" Justin asked.

"Terry Thomas, chief cook," the guy said. "Who are *you*?"

"We're your assistants," Justin said.

Terry smiled. "Welcome to Camp Run-a-Muck."

CHAPTER

9

We didn't get to talk to Terry long because he said he had to go call his girlfriend, Doris, who worked at a camp on the other side of the lake.

"I have one last question," he said. "Either of you know how to cook?"

We shook our heads.

"Figures." Terry left, and the bunkhouse door banged shut behind him.

"Why does everyone keep asking if we know how to cook?" Justin asked me.

"Gee, Justin, I can't imagine," I replied as I walked into the bathroom and looked around. The yellow tiles on the walls were covered with graffiti. Instead of a string, a rope ending in a loop hung from a lightbulb.

"Uh, is it my imagination, or is that a noose?" Justin asked.

"Maybe they use it to hang guys who can't cook," I said.

"Please be excusing me," a voice said. "Are either of you being at work here?"

Justin and I turned to find a big guy with darkly tanned skin standing in the entrance to the bathroom. He must've been six-and-a-half-feet tall, with all the major muscle groups. I couldn't quite tell where he was from. His skin had a dark hue, and his long, straight, black hair was pulled into a ponytail. He was wearing a sheepskin vest and hat. Beads of perspiration dotted his forehead.

"We're not sure," Justin said.

The big guy scowled. "Sorry, but I am not understanding you. Either you are working here or you are not."

"That's what we're trying to decide," Justin said.

The big guy wiped his forehead with the back of his hand. "Would you be knowing if this place is being called the bunkhouse?"

"This is it," I said. "By the way, I'm Lucas Harmon."

"I am Bag Jammer," the guy said. Then he turned and yelled something outside. A second later half a dozen smaller guys entered the bunkhouse in single file carrying duffel bags on their heads. None of them was big as Bag, but they all had dark complexions and were wearing sheepskin clothes. They looked young, but I couldn't tell how young.

Bag Jammer turned to Justin and me again. "For weeks we are being on boats to travel here," he said.

"From where?" Justin asked.

"We are being from the mountains of Tibet," Bag replied. He pointed at his companions. "They are being orphan Sherpas. The owner of this camp is being kind to take them in for the summer. To bring them here is being my job. Now I am being done and I will go back to the mountains. Here it is being too hot. I am not being used to this climate."

"What's an orphan Sherpa?" Justin asked.

Bag scowled. "You are not knowing what is an orphan?"

"Sure I do," Justin said. "An orphan is some kid whose parents have died. I just don't know what an orphan *Sherpa* is."

Bag looked at me as if he was wondering if I was as dumb as my friend.

"Sherpas are from Tibet," I said. "They're famous for climbing mountains."

"So an orphan Sherpa is a mountain-climbing kid from Tibet whose parents have croaked?" Justin speculated.

"This is being correct," Bag said.

"Are you a Sherpa, too?" Justin asked.

"Yes," said Bag. "Now I will be finding the owner of the camp. He will be giving me a plane ticket back to my country."

Bag turned and ordered the orphan Sherpas to unpack their duffel bags.

"This is getting pretty interesting," Justin said.

"We're working for The Blob who sucks ketchup, and Terry, who's a dead-fly freak. And our roommates are half a dozen orphan Sherpas."

I looked at my watch. It was three o'clock. "Time for our meeting in the kitchen. Let's go see what the rest of the inmates in this nuthouse are like."

We left the bunkhouse. As we walked back toward the dining hall and kitchen, I noticed a big yellow house up on a hill behind the camp. It was surrounded by gardens of colorful flowers.

"Wonder who lives there," I said.

"Probably the owner of the camp," Justin guessed.

We went into the dining hall and down to the kitchen. Inside there were a bunch of big chrome industrial-size refrigerators and stoves. Huge industrial-size pots and pans hung from racks over flat metal counters. Justin and I sat down. Terry, the chief cook, was talking on the wall phone.

"Of course I love you, Doris," he said. "I'll come see you tonight. Yes, I *promise*."

Bag Jammer came in, followed by the orphan Sherpas, who seemed to go everywhere in single file.

Justin tore open a bag of red pistachio nuts he'd brought from home and offered me some. "Knock, knock."

"Who's there?" I said.

"Cash."

"Cash who?"

"No, thanks, I prefer pistachios," he said. "Get it? Cash who, like cashew?"

I sighed. "That's *almost* funny, Justin."

"Really?" Justin brightened. "From you, that's a compliment."

The kitchen door opened again and Amanda, the pretty girl with the blond hair, came in. Justin grew quiet and got a strange, dazed look on his face.

Then the ketchup-sucking Blob came in. When he saw Terry on the phone, the lines between his eyes deepened.

"Are you talking to your girlfriend again?" The Blob growled.

Terry quickly hung up the receiver.

"That's better," The Blob said. He turned to the rest of us. "Okay, everyone. I have good news and bad news. The bad news is that we're short-staffed. That means you'll all have to work harder and longer."

"What about the other cook?" Terry asked.

"He couldn't make it," The Blob replied.

"You mean, it's just me and these two assistants?" Terry said.

"That's right," The Blob replied.

"But they don't even know how to cook," Terry complained.

"Then teach 'em," said The Blob. "The campers will be here tomorrow."

"Why are the orphan Sherpas in the kitchen, Uncle Bob?" asked Amanda.

"Did you hear that?" Justin whispered. "She called him *Uncle* Bob. She must be part of the family that owns this place."

"They'll be working in the kitchen this summer," said The Blob.

"But you told my parents the Sherpas could be campers," Amanda said. "You said you felt sorry for them and would let them come for free."

"Sorry," The Blob said with a shrug.

Bag Jammer raised his hand. "May I ask what is being done about my plane ticket to Tibet?"

The Blob shook his head. "Never got around to buying it. Sorry."

"I am not understanding," Bag said. "What am I to do?"

"I guess you're stuck here," The Blob said.

A shocked silence fell over the kitchen. Finally, Justin raised his hand. "You said you had good news and bad news. But so far you've only given us bad news. What's the good news?"

The Blob scratched his head. "I forgot."

CHAPTER

10

That night, Terry taught Justin, Bag, and me to cook. He'd decided to make Bag an assistant cook, too.

"Stir!" he shouted at us. He was sitting on a metal table, plucking the wings off a fly.

Justin and I were standing at a stove stirring two huge pots. Justin's was full of tomato sauce. Mine was full of spaghetti. We were wearing white aprons and stirring with big metal spoons. The heat from the stoves was making us sweat.

Bag was standing at a broad stainless-steel counter, chopping tomatoes. He had to stay away from the stoves because he couldn't stand the heat.

"This is not being right," Bag grumbled. "The camp owner is being tricky with me. I should be going back to the mountains to be leading expeditions."

"Sorry, Baggy," Terry said. "It looks like we're all stuck here for one reason or another. Know what this place is like? A Venus flytrap. If you're a fly it looks so nice and inviting. You just can't wait to land. Then, *pow*! You're stuck. You know how a Venus flytrap digests its prey?"

Justin and I shook our heads.

"It traps the fly and closes around it," Terry said. "Then it's got this *enzyme* that digests that fly *alive*. Imagine that, dudes. You see your body *dissolve* before your own eyes. First your wings go, then your legs. Then your body slowly starts to turn into mush. It's like being dropped into a vat of slow-acting acid ... hey! Keep stirring!"

Justin and I kept stirring.

"Why are we cooking dinner now if we're not gonna serve it until tomorrow night?" I asked.

"I like to plan ahead," Terry said and pulled another wing off a fly. He had a butterfly net. Every time he finished pulling the wings off one fly, he'd put it in a jar and then catch another with the net.

"But won't the spaghetti be totally limp and disgusting by tomorrow night?" Justin asked.

"This is camp, flybrain," Terry replied. "The food is *supposed* to be limp and disgusting."

When Terry wasn't catching flies, he was on the wall phone with his girlfriend, Doris. Or he was giving us rules.

"Rule number one," Terry said to us. "You stay off that phone. The only one who uses it is me."

29

Justin, Bag, and I nodded.

"Rule number two," said Terry. "Anytime anyone wants to know where I am, I'm at the store. Got that?"

"What if you're here?" Justin asked.

Terry rolled his eyes in disbelief. "If I'm here, they won't be asking you where I am, right?"

"Oh, yeah." Justin nodded sheepishly.

Around ten o'clock the skinny guy with the curly brown hair came in. I remembered him from that afternoon. He was the one who carried The Blob's golf bag.

"Mr. Kirby wants an egg sandwich on toast and french fries," he said. "And a chocolate milk shake for dessert."

"Coming right up." Terry put a couple of slices of bread in the industrial-size toaster and started to cook up some eggs and fries.

"You see a box of frozen Milky Ways in there?" the skinny guy asked, pointing at one of the industrial-size refrigerators.

Terry shook his head.

"Darn," said the guy. "I left 'em there last summer. Someone must've taken them during the winter."

"Wait a minute," I said. "Did you say you were here *last* year?"

The guy nodded.

I introduced myself and offered him my hand. "What's your name?"

"Brad Schmook," he answered. His handshake was really limp, and he stared down at the floor.

"So what's the story here?" I asked. "Is this place cool or not?"

Brad shrugged. "Sure, it's cool. Why wouldn't it be?"

"Well, for one thing, they didn't hire enough people, so we all have to work extra hard," I said.

"That happens at every camp," Brad said. "Don't worry about it. Mr. Kirby will hire more workers."

A couple of minutes later the egg sandwich and fries were ready. Terry took out a key and opened one of the industrial-size refrigerators. It was the only one with a lock on it. He got out some milk and chocolate ice cream. He made the milk shake.

"How come that refrigerator has a lock?" I asked.

"It's Mr. Kirby's private fridge," Terry said. "No one else is allowed to take food from it."

When the food was ready, Brad took it and left.

"What was that all about?" I asked.

"What the fat man wants, the fat man gets," Terry replied.

CHAPTER

11

The steam from the boiling spaghetti rose into my face. Sweat dripped down my forehead. I had to wipe my brow with the sleeve of my T-shirt. Terry plucked the wings off another fly and dropped it into the jar. By now, the bottom of the jar was crawling with wingless flies.

"Knock, knock," Justin said.

"What?" Terry frowned.

"I said, 'knock, knock.' Like a knock, knock joke," Justin explained.

"Oh, okay." Terry sighed. "Who's there?"

"Pasta," said Justin.

"Pasta who?"

"Isn't it pasta our bedtime?"

Terry frowned. "Your jokes are almost as bad as your cooking." He looked at his watch. "It's pretty late. You can go back to the bunkhouse."

"Aren't you going back to the bunkhouse, too?" Justin asked.

"Naw, I gotta go see Doris," Terry said.

Justin and I turned off the stoves. Bag cleaned the counters. Terry put the jar of flies in one of the big refrigerators.

We left the kitchen and walked through the dark back to the bunkhouse. The moon was out, and the night air felt fresh and cool.

"So what do you call a plant that catches bread?" Justin asked.

"You got me," I replied with a shrug.

"A Venus *rye*trap."

I had to groan. "Good thing I'm too tired to really care."

"Yeah, me, too," Justin said. "Who would have thought cooking could be such hard work? I can't wait to hit the sack. I'm gonna sleep like a rock tonight."

Groof! Groof! A dog barked somewhere in the dark.

"Whoa!" Justin froze. "That dog sounds big."

"And he is not being of a friendly nature," Bag added.

The barking seemed to come from the big yellow house on the hill. The lights were on inside.

"I bet it's the guard dog for that house," I said.

"So what has four legs and one arm?" Justin asked.

Bag and I shook our heads.

"A pit bull leaving a playground," Justin said. "Let's stay away from that place."

We went into the bunkhouse. The lights were out. We walked quietly past the sleeping orphan Sherpas toward the back, where our bunks were. Just then I noticed a dark figure hovering near our cubbies. The guy must've heard our footsteps, because he straightened up and backed away.

It was Brad Schmook, the skinny kid with the curly brown hair.

"Can I help you?" I asked.

Brad shook his head. But his eyes kept shifting around.

"What were you doing around our cubbies?" Justin asked.

"Uh, nothing," he said. "I was looking for my bunk. Guess I got confused."

Brad started off toward his bunk. In the dark, Justin and I shared a look.

"I'm not sure I trust that guy," Justin said in a low voice.

CHAPTER

12

The next morning Terry woke us at dawn, and we spent the whole day in that hot kitchen. Every couple of hours Brad Schmook would appear with a special order from The Blob. Terry would get the food from The Blob's private refrigerator. He made him scrambled eggs and french toast for breakfast. A roast beef hero at lunch. A cheeseburger and fries in the middle of the afternoon. Steak at dinner. Terry always prepared The Blob's orders personally.

"The only reason the fat man doesn't eat twenty-four hours a day is that he has to take time to play golf and sleep," Terry grumbled, wiping the sweat off his forehead.

"What's the story with that golf course?" Justin asked.

"It's the fat man's private course," Terry said. "He invites his friends to play there all the time."

"I've never heard of anyone having a private golf course," Justin said.

Terry just smirked.

All afternoon, buses and cars arrived bringing campers. Every time we looked outside we saw kids carrying duffel bags and trunks into cabins. Meanwhile, Terry spent most of the afternoon on the phone with Doris.

"Of course I love you," he said. "Of course I'll come see you tonight . . . what? Yes, I *promise*."

"Hey, Terry, don't we get a break?" Justin asked at one point. "We've been working nonstop since six this morning."

"Okay, take ten minutes," he said.

"Come on," Justin said to me. "I need something cold to drink."

We went out into the dining hall and headed down toward the canteen. Brad Schmook was leaning on the counter, talking to Amanda.

"Hey, come on," he was saying. "It'll be a beautiful night for a walk in the woods. What do you say?"

Amanda shook her head. "No, thanks."

"Why not?" Brad asked.

"I hardly know you," said Amanda.

"That's the whole point," Brad said. "We'll get to know each other during the walk."

Amanda turned and saw us. She smiled shyly,

revealing her even, white teeth. "Hi."

Justin's mouth fell open, but no words came out. I'd never seen him act like that before.

"Got a couple of Cokes?" I asked.

"Sure thing." Amanda got out a couple of cans.

Brad had a sour look on his face. He probably didn't like the fact that we'd interrupted him.

"How's life in the kitchen?" he asked us.

"Hot," Justin said.

He turned back to Amanda. "I have to go caddie for Mr. Kirby. He's playing golf with some friends this afternoon. Don't forget what we talked about, okay?"

Amanda nodded and looked back at Justin and me. "So what's for dinner tonight, guys?"

"Spaghetti we made yesterday," I said. "It's really gross. If I were you, I'd make other plans."

"Like what?" she asked.

"Pizza," I said.

Justin's eyes widened nervously. "You mean, sneak out of camp?"

"It's not *sneaking* out of camp," I said. "We'll be finished with work for the day. We can do what we want."

"Well, I don't know," Justin said. "We just got here. I don't want to get into trouble."

"What do you think?" I asked Amanda.

"I think pizza sounds a lot better than yesterday's spaghetti," she said.

CHAPTER

13

At dinnertime the dining hall was filled with boys and girls wearing light blue Camp Run-a-Muck T-shirts. We reheated the spaghetti we'd made the day before. The orphan Sherpas served it on paper plates along with green beans and salad.

Terry spent most of the time on the phone with Doris.

"Honey, you *know* I love you," he was saying. "I'll *always* love you. Of course I'll come see you tonight."

By seven P.M. we were done. The campers finished dinner and left the dining hall. The orphan Sherpas finished washing down the tables and floors.

"Know what's amazing?" I asked Justin.

"What?"

"They ate that stuff," I said. "And not one kid complained."

Justin shrugged. "Hey, it was their first meal. What do they know?"

"Congratulations, guys," Terry said as we pulled off our sweat-soaked, stained aprons. "You just completed your first fourteen-hour day. Finish cleaning up and I'll see you tomorrow morning at dawn."

He left.

"Where's he going?" Justin asked.

"To see his girlfriend, where else?" I answered.

A little while later Justin and I turned off the kitchen lights and left the dining hall. The sun was behind the trees, throwing long shadows across the camp lawn.

"Underwear raid!" someone shouted. A bunch of ten-year-old girls raced past with a pair of boy's boxer shorts tied to a stick like a flag.

"You know," Justin said with a yawn, "except for a couple of minutes this morning, I don't think I saw the sun all day."

"What a *great* summer experience," I said with a smirk.

Then we heard a sound like a loud cough, followed by a splash.

Justin stopped and looked around. "Sounds like someone just lost their dinner."

"Over there." I pointed into the shadows where a younger kid was bent over, holding his stomach.

"Hey, you okay?" I called.

The kid straightened up and nodded. Then he came toward us, wiping his mouth on his arm. He was wearing a dirty Camp Run-a-Muck T-shirt. He had red hair, freckles, and big ears.

"You *sure* you're okay?" I asked.

"Yeah," the kid said. "I barf a lot. It's because I have a weak stomach. Didn't you think dinner was gross?"

Justin and I shared a guilty look. After all, we'd cooked that dinner.

"What's your name?" I asked.

"Ralphie," he said.

"Listen, Ralphie," I said. "How would you like a slice of pizza?"

Ralphie's eye widened. "You serious?"

"It'll take a while," I said. "Think you can wait?"

"You bet," Ralphie said eagerly.

"Okay," I said. "See you later."

CHAPTER 14

"I don't know about this," Justin muttered nervously a few minutes later. We were in the bunkhouse, changing out of our work clothes.

"Don't you want to go have pizza with Amanda?" I asked.

"Well, sure," Justin said.

"Then don't sweat it," I said.

"Yeah, I guess," Justin said with a shrug.

Just then Brad came by. "You guys going somewhere?"

"Lucas wants to go down the road to that pizza place," Justin told him. "You think that's okay?"

"Sure, it's cool," Brad said.

"You don't think we'll get in trouble?" Justin asked.

"I doubt it," Brad said.

"See?" I said.

* * *

As soon as it was dark, we went outside and met Amanda. The three of us took the trail through the woods that led to the road. Amanda told us that her parents were Christian missionaries in Tibet.

"I'm really upset about the orphan Sherpas," she said. "Uncle Bob promised my parents they'd have a great summer. I can't believe he only wanted them so they could work in the camp kitchen."

"Is The Blob, er, I mean, Mr. Kirby, *really* your uncle?" I asked.

"No," Amanda said. "He's my step-uncle, actually. I never really knew his side of the family."

"Looks like you were lucky," Justin said.

"Until now," said Amanda.

Soon we got to the road.

Groof! Groof! Groof! We could hear the sound of barking in the distance.

"It's that dog again," Justin said. "He sounds really mean."

"That's Uncle Bob's dog," Amanda said. "You don't have to worry. He keeps him in a pen behind the house."

We kept walking. There wasn't a car in sight. The road was lined on both sides with tall, dark pines.

"Gee, it's dark," Justin muttered.

"Look up," I said.

Directly above us, stars shimmered in the clear night sky.

"Wow, I've never seen stars shine so bright," Justin gasped in wonder.

"That's because there're no other lights around," I said.

"*Ahhhhh!*" Just then Amanda let out a scream.

CHAPTER
15

Amanda threw her arms around my neck. I could feel her trembling with fear.

"What happened?" Justin asked.

"I saw something," Amanda gasped. "I mean, someone. At least, I think it was a someone."

"Where?" I asked.

"There." Amanda pointed down the road.

I looked and didn't see anything.

"He ran off into the woods when I screamed," Amanda said.

"What'd he look like?" Justin asked.

"He looked like a hippie," she said. "I think he had a beard and long hair."

Justin and I shared a knowing glance.

"Was he carrying a sack?" I asked.

"And a stick?" added Justin.

"Yes!" Amanda stared at us in amazement. "How did you know?"

"We saw him the other day," I said.

"They call him Roadkill Man," Justin said.

"Why do they call him that?" Amanda asked.

Justin and I shared another glance.

"Believe me," Justin said. "You don't want to know."

"Come on," I said. "Let's go see if he's still around."

Amanda grabbed my arm and held me back. "You're not serious, are you?"

"Sure," I said, peering into the dark woods. All I could see were tree trunks. "Hey, Roadkill Man," I called. "You in there?"

No answer came back. All we could hear was the distant barking of The Blob's dog.

"He must've split," Justin said.

"Wait," I said. "I thought I saw something move." I took a step toward the trees.

"You're not going into the woods in the dark, are you?" Justin asked.

"Why not?" I asked.

"Because it's creepy," Justin said. "I mean, there could be bears in there. Or man-eating chipmunks or something."

"I'll take my chances," I said. I took another step toward the woods. It was doubly dark in there. Not only was it night, but every shred of starlight was blocked by the treetops.

"Lucas, don't," Amanda pleaded.

But I stepped off the road and into the trees.

It was so dark, I couldn't see my hand in front of my face.

Except for the distant barks of The Blob's dog, it was dead quiet.

Crick . . .

I heard something that sounded like a footstep.

"That you, Roadkill Man?" I whispered.

Crick . . . crack . . .

I followed the sound with my eyes. Suddenly I thought I saw something. Just a shadow in human form standing about thirty feet away. Then that eye-burning odor reached my nose.

"Roadkill Man?" I whispered, wiping the tears out of my eyes.

He raised his hand with the index and middle fingers up — giving me the peace sign.

I did the same. "Right," I said. "Peace to you, too."

"Hey, Lucas!" Justin suddenly shouted. "You find him?"

I spun around and told him to quiet down. But when I turned back, Roadkill Man was gone.

CHAPTER

16

"**W**hat happened?" Justin asked when I got back to the road.

"I saw him, but he freaked and ran away," I said.

"Why did you want to talk to him?" Amanda asked.

"I just did," I said with a shrug. "People like that interest me. I mean, don't you wonder why he lives out in the woods all by himself?"

"No," Justin said.

We began walking toward Log Cabin Pizza.

"Why do cannibals like to eat at truck stops?" Justin asked.

"Uh, because truck stops serve truckers?" Amanda guessed.

Justin gazed at her in awe. "You are incredible!"

Amanda smiled shyly. "Thanks. But you know what the trouble is with cannibal jokes?"

Justin and I shook our heads.

"They're always in bad taste," Amanda said.

I laughed.

"I don't get it." Justin frowned. "Why are they always in bad taste?"

"Cannibals, dummy," I said. "Bad taste."

"Oh! Now I get it!" Justin smiled sheepishly.

When we got to Log Cabin Pizza, we ordered a pizza and some Cokes from the same waitress we'd had the last time.

"You kids from the camp?" she asked as she served our pizza.

"We work there," Justin said.

The waitress looked surprised. "And they let you out?"

"We sort of snuck out," Justin said.

"Where are you headed for next?" she asked.

Justin, Amanda, and I shared a puzzled look.

"Back to camp," I said.

"That's a first," the waitress said. "Usually when someone who works there stops here, they're running away as fast as they can. I hear Bob Kirby's not very nice. They say he's a real slave driver."

Justin, Amanda, and I shared a knowing look.

"But maybe I'm wrong," the waitress said. "I mean, you kids got out and you're going back."

She left to take another order.

"I wish she was wrong," Justin groaned. "But I have a feeling she's right."

We finished our pizza and got an extra slice for

Ralphie. Then we started back to camp. Amanda seemed a little nervous.

"I hope we don't run into Roadkill Man again," she said.

Grrrrrrrrrrrrrr . . .

Suddenly we heard the sound of a fierce growl behind us. All three of us froze. My heart started to race, and I could feel the hair on the back of my neck stand up. Next to me, Justin was white with fear.

"Think it's Roadkill Man?" Justin whispered.

"I wish," I whispered back.

CHAPTER
17

We slowly turned around. Standing behind us was The Blob, with a nasty-looking smile on his face. At his feet was a big, fat, black and white bulldog with pointy sharp teeth.

Grrrrrrrrrrrrr . . . he growled. Long white globs of saliva hung from his jowls.

The Blob reached out and grabbed Ralphie's slice of pizza out of my hands. He practically finished the whole thing in one bite. "Looks like you went out for pizza, huh?"

Justin and I swallowed nervously and nodded.

"The first full day of camp isn't even over, and you've already broken a major rule," The Blob said, his cheeks bulging with pizza.

"What rule?" Justin asked.

"You're not allowed to leave the camp without asking me first," said The Blob.

Grrrrrrrrrrrrr . . . growled The Blob Dog.

"We didn't know we had to ask you for permission," Justin said.

"*Uuuurp!*" The Blob let out a long, loud belch. "Not knowing the rules is no excuse," he grumbled. "You'll both have to be punished for this. No day off this week."

"But — " Justin began.

"No buts!" The Blob yelled. "Get back to camp! Now!"

"Wait, Uncle Bob," said Amanda. "You punished them, but what about me? Don't I get punished, too?"

"I'm going to let you go, Amanda," The Blob said. "I'm sure you wouldn't have done this by yourself. These two boys were a bad influence on you."

"That's not true, Uncle Bob," Amanda said. "I wanted to go get pizza."

"Just go back to camp!" The Blob yelled.

GRROOOFFFF! The Blob Dog growled and lunged. If The Blob hadn't pulled back on his leash, he would have gotten one of us.

Amanda, Justin, and I walked back to camp in the dark.

"I'm really sorry, guys," Amanda said. "He won't punish me because I'm his niece, but I deserve it as much as you."

"The trouble is, we *don't* deserve it," I said. "He never told us we weren't allowed to leave the camp without permission."

"I'll talk to him tomorrow," Amanda said. "Maybe when he's calmed down he'll change his mind."

"Don't bother," I said. "You're not going to get him to change his mind."

Justin and I said good-bye to Amanda. We got back to the bunkhouse and went in. The lights were off, and everyone was asleep. We walked through the shadows to our bunk.

"No day off this week," Justin muttered quietly. "What a bummer."

"Yeah," I had to agree.

"Just our luck that we should run into The Blob on the way home," Justin said. "I mean, what was he doing out on the road at this time of night?"

I was wondering the same thing.

The next morning we made breakfast for the camp. Justin fed bread into the industrial-size toast-making machine and stacked it on trays for the orphan Sherpas to take out to the campers. When Bag and the orphan Sherpas got too hot, they would stand in the industrial-size freezers to cool off.

I reheated the day-old scrambled eggs in the industrial-size microwave oven.

"Hey, Lucas," Justin said. "Why were screams coming from the kitchen?"

"You got me." I shrugged.

"The cook was beating the eggs."

I sighed. Terry was on the phone with Doris.

"But, baby," he was saying. "I just saw you last night ... okay, okay, I'll come by again tonight ... yes, I *promise*."

"What's the Abominable Snowman's favorite lunch?" Justin asked.

"I don't know," I said.

"Chili dogs," he said. "Chili. Like *chilly*. Get it?"

No one laughed.

"Lucas," Bag Jammer said. "Is it not bothering you to be listening to these jokes all the time?"

"Sometimes," I said, as I stirred a big vat of orange juice. "But it keeps me from going stir-crazy."

Bag laughed. "*Stir*-crazy? Now, *that* is being a joke. Yes?"

"Hey, what about me?" Justin sounded hurt that he'd been left out.

"You are being okay, Justin," said Bag. "I am just wishing you would not be telling so many bad jokes."

Everyone chuckled. As Justin handed a tray of toast to an orphan Sherpa, a shadow seemed to come over the kitchen. It was The Blob. Brad Schmook followed behind him, carrying the big black golf bag.

"How many times have I told you to stay off the phone?" The Blob yelled at Terry.

Terry quickly hung up the receiver.

The Blob turned to the rest of us. "What are you smiling about?"

Everyone stopped smiling.

"Maybe you assistant cooks don't have enough to do," The Blob grumbled. "Maybe I ought to give you some more work."

Just then an orphan Sherpa accidentally tilted the tray of toast. A bunch of slices slid off and fell to the floor. The whole kitchen was silent as The Blob stared at the slices of toast on the floor.

"Well?" The Blob demanded.

The orphan Sherpa looked up at him and trembled with fear.

"You just gonna leave it there?" The Blob asked angrily.

The orphan Sherpa's eyes darted left and right in panic. He looked really scared.

"Please be excusing me, Mr. Kirby," Bag Jammer said.

"Did I ask you to speak?" The Blob shouted at him.

"No, but — "

"Then, *shut up!*" The Blob screamed.

The orphan Sherpa was still shaking.

"He doesn't understand what you're saying," I said.

The Blob narrowed his eyes at me as if he was going to yell again. But then he changed his mind and turned to Bag. "Tell him to pick up that toast."

Bag spoke to the orphan Sherpa, who picked up the toast and started to walk toward a garbage can.

"Wait!" The Blob bellowed. "What's he doing?"

"He is throwing it out," explained Bag.

"I didn't tell him to do that," growled The Blob. "Tell him to put it back on the tray. I've got a dining hall full of hungry campers out there."

"But this toast has been falling to the floor," Bag said.

"So?" The Blob turned to Terry. "Aren't you keeping the floor clean?"

Terry nodded. The Blob turned back to Bag. "See? There's nothing wrong with that toast."

"You are not to be serious," said Bag.

"Oh, yeah?" The Blob's eyebrows rose. "You want to see how serious I can be? Watch."

The Blob reached for one of the slices that had fallen on the floor and handed it to Brad Schmook. "Eat it."

CHAPTER

19

Brad made a face. Then he nibbled a corner of the toast.

"The whole thing!" The Blob ordered.

Brad sighed and stuffed the whole slice into his mouth.

"So?" The Blob arched a fat eyebrow.

"Tastes fine to me," said Brad.

The Blob put his hand on the orphan Sherpa's shoulder and shoved him toward the swinging doors that led to the dining hall. "Now get out there!"

The orphan Sherpa stumbled and almost dropped the toast again. He disappeared out the doors.

"You don't have to push them around," I said.

The whole kitchen came to a halt. The only sound was the grumbling of the refrigerator and the humming of the microwave.

The Blob turned to me with an incredulous look on his face. "What did you just say?"

"You don't have to push them around," I repeated.

The Blob's face turned red. His meaty hands turned into fists the size of boxing gloves. He took a step toward me. I picked up my fists.

"Uh, excuse me, Mr. Kirby." Terry quickly stepped between us.

"What do you want?" The Blob growled.

"I just want to remind you that you only have one cook and three assistants," Terry said. "If I lose this assistant I won't be able to feed this camp. It won't be long before all those campers start calling home to their parents to complain that they're starving to death."

The thought of a bunch of angry parents screaming that their kids were starving seemed to calm down The Blob. He unclenched his fists, but stuck his big fat red face close to mine.

"Listen, punk," he growled. His breath was so foul, it made my eyes water. "No one talks to me like that. Understand? One more word out of you and you'll be scrubbing this floor with your tongue."

The Blob turned and left. Brad hurried after him.

CHAPTER

20

That night in the bunkhouse I packed my backpack. A small crowd gathered around me. Justin was there, along with Bag and some of the orphan Sherpas. Terry was across the lake visiting Doris.

"What are you doing?" Justin asked.

"What does it look like?" I replied.

"Packing up to leave is looking like what you are doing," said Bag.

"You got it," I said.

"But you can't leave," Justin said. "We just got here."

"Sorry." I shook my head.

"If you please, Lucas," Bag whispered. "I have decided to be seeking revenge against this Blob. You should be staying to enjoy this."

"Sorry, Bag, I'm not interested," I said. "But I wish you luck."

Seeing that they couldn't change my mind, the

guys began to drift away. Soon, only Justin was left. "You can't do this to me," he said in a low voice.

"I'm not doing anything to you," I said. "I'm just getting out of here. You can come, too."

Justin shook his head. "I can't."

"Sure you can," I said. "Pack up and leave with me tonight. In the dark. Let The Blob try to figure out how to feed everyone himself."

"I can't," Justin repeated.

"Of course you can," I said.

Justin bowed his head sadly. "You don't understand."

"What are you talking about, Justin?" I asked. "We'll just go. The Blob can't stop us. What's your problem?"

Justin stepped close to me. His face was turning red. I could see that it wasn't easy for him to say what came next. "My problem is . . . Amanda."

"Huh?" I didn't understand.

"I can't leave her," Justin said.

I stared at him like he'd lost his mind. "Are you serious?"

"Shh." He pressed a finger to his lips. "Keep it quiet, will you? I don't want everyone to know."

"I don't get it," I said.

"Neither do I," Justin said with a shrug. "But I just can't go now, man."

"Does she know you feel this way?" I asked.

"I don't know." Justin shrugged. "Maybe. It's hard

to tell. But I gotta stay. Only, I'll never make it here without you."

It was hard to believe, but I knew Justin was telling me the truth. I took a deep breath and let it out slowly. "Okay, Justin, for you I'll stay."

CHAPTER
21

The next morning after breakfast, Justin and I took a break and went to get a couple of Cokes at the canteen. A bunch of campers ran past, carrying one kid who was wrapped in toilet paper from head to toe.

"Dump him in the mud!" the campers were chanting. "Dump him in the mud!"

"Don't hear much from the counselors at this camp, do you?" Justin said.

"Nope," I replied.

The line of campers waiting to buy stuff at the canteen stretched halfway across the dining hall.

"I don't get it," Justin said. "These kids just had breakfast. They can't be hungry already."

Just then I noticed Ralphie, the red-haired kid who'd barfed up the spaghetti dinner two nights before. He was staring at me. "Hey, you!"

I went over. "Hey, Ralphie, how's it going?"

"Lousy," Ralphie said. "I waited up all night for

that slice of pizza you promised me. What happened?"

I explained how I'd gotten the slice for him, but then The Blob caught us and ate it.

"That stinks," Ralphie muttered.

"Listen, Ralphie," I said. "How come you're on line for the canteen?"

"I'm starving," Ralphie said.

"But you just had breakfast," said Justin.

"Are you nuts?" Ralphie asked. "I *looked* at breakfast and nearly barfed. That french toast was growing *green slime*. It looked like it was made last week."

"Naw, it was only made yesterday," Justin said.

I poked him in the ribs and whispered, "You're not supposed to tell them that!"

"Anyway, I gotta get something to eat," Ralphie said.

Justin and I walked up to the front of the line. Amanda was selling candy to kids at a feverish pace. Brad Schmook was leaning on the counter, eating Raisinets. "You ever tried canoeing on the lake at night under the moonlight?" he asked Amanda.

She shook her head as she handed a kid a bag of licorice.

"Oh, wow, it's the best," Brad said. "How about you and I go out tonight and I'll show you?"

"I'd love to, Brad," Amanda said. "But I'm afraid I have to write a letter to my parents."

Brad placed the box of Raisinets against his lips. He tilted his head back and let a bunch of candy slide into his mouth. "Aw, forget about your parents."

"We'll do it another time, okay?" Amanda said.

Brad was about to say something else, but then he noticed Justin and me. "I'll talk to you later, Amanda." He left.

"Are you really going to go canoeing with Brad?" Justin asked Amanda.

"No," Amanda replied as she sold a camper a box of Whoppers.

"So how's business?" I asked.

"Amazing," Amanda said. "I'm busy selling candy day and night. The campers all say the same thing: The food is so horrible here, they can only survive by eating candy."

"I wonder if The Blob does it on purpose," Justin speculated. "Just to make more money."

"I bet he does," Amanda said.

Justin and I got a couple of Cokes and went back to the kitchen. Terry was gone, and everyone was sitting around Bag.

"Hello, my friends," Bag said when he saw us. "I am being glad you are here. We are planning to seek revenge against this Blob. Any suggestions?"

"Let's balance a big pail of tomato sauce over the door to the kitchen," Justin suggested. "When The Blob walks in, the can will tip over and dump the sauce on his head."

"That's a great idea," I said. "Except The Blob will know exactly who did it."

"Lucas is being right," said Bag. "Is anyone else having any other ideas?"

One of the orphan Sherpas said something in Nepali.

"What did he say?" Justin asked.

"He is saying into the laundry we should be sneaking and tying into knots this Blob's underwear," said Bag.

"No way!" Justin gasped. "I wouldn't touch The Blob's underwear if you paid me."

"Besides," I said, "how do we know if he even *wears* underwear?"

Just then Brad came in. "Hey, what's going on?" he asked when he saw us all sitting around.

"Perhaps you can be helping us," Bag said to him. "You are recalling how this Blob made you eat from the floor toast? Would you not be liking to seek revenge for this?"

"Uh . . ." Brad frowned. "Sure I would."

"Can you be giving suggestions for this revenge?" Bag asked.

Brad grinned. "I sure can." Then he told us that the one thing The Blob loved more than anything else was the golf course. "The eighteenth hole is his favorite. It ends right behind his house. If you guys really want to get him, you should go tear up the green."

That night after lights-out, Justin and Bag snuck out of the bunkhouse. I went to sleep.

Someone woke me in the middle of the night. "Lucas! Wake up, man!"

I opened my eyes. Justin was crouched beside me. He was breathing hard, and his forehead glistened with sweat. "Come on, you gotta help me," he whispered. "Bag's hurt."

"What happened?" I asked as I sat up.

"I'll tell you on the way," Justin hissed. "We have to hurry."

I got dressed and quietly followed Justin outside.

"It was a total bust," Justin said as we hurried along in the dark. "We got to the eighteenth hole. It was dark, and we couldn't see. All of a sudden it attacked us."

"What attacked you?" I asked.

"The Blob Dog," Justin said.

"What was he doing on the golf course?" I asked.

"I don't know," Justin said. "All I know is that he came after us, and we ran. Bag tripped over a tree root. He twisted his ankle pretty bad."

We found Bag sitting under a tree in the dark. He was clutching his ankle. Even in the dark I could see that it was badly swollen.

"Is it broken?" I asked.

"I am not thinking so." Bag grimaced. "I am thinking it is being badly twisted."

"We gotta get him back to the bunkhouse before The Blob catches us," said Justin.

Justin and I helped Bag up. He put an arm over each of our shoulders and we helped him hobble back to the bunkhouse. Inside, Bag lay down on a bunk and we wrapped his ankle in wet towels full of ice.

"That should help the swelling go down," I whispered. "With any luck, you'll be able to hobble around in the morning."

"Thanks to you, my friends," Bag said.

Justin and I went to our bunks.

"What a bummer, man," Justin whispered as we got into our beds. "I mean, it was just bad luck to pick the one night when the dog was there."

"Yeah," I said. But I had to wonder: Was it *just* bad luck? Or was there more to it?

The next morning the swelling on Bag's ankle had gone down. We found a tree branch he could use as a cane, and he was able to hobble around.

We were in the middle of making breakfast when The Blob came into the kitchen with a big grin on his face. He was wearing his golf clothes and carrying a golf club over his shoulder. "So," he said, "I trust everyone slept well last night."

No one answered. The Blob walked over to Bag. "Something wrong with your foot, Jammer?"

"Not to be worrying," Bag answered. "It is just being a little twisted."

"Really?" The Blob acted surprised. "That's odd. It was fine last night after dinner. I can't imagine how you could have twisted it between here and the bunkhouse."

Bag didn't reply. The Blob looked around at all of us. But he wasn't smiling anymore. "All right, listen up, you twerps!" he growled. "Some of you may think you can get me. But it's never gonna happen, understand? No matter what you try, I'll always know about it ahead of time."

The Blob picked up the golf club he was carrying and banged it against Bag's bad ankle.

"Ow!" Bag cried out in pain and grabbed his foot.

"Consider yourself lucky," The Blob snarled at him. "Next time I'll make sure it's broken."

He stomped out of the kitchen.

"Did you hear what he said?" Justin gasped. "He knew about the plan! It was a setup! But how could he know?"

"Someone has been telling him," Bag said.

But who?

CHAPTER

24

We finished cooking breakfast and took a short break. Justin and I hung out with Bag.

"How's the ankle?" I asked.

"It is not feeling good," Bag said. "It is hit hard by this Blob."

"I've got a joke that will cheer you up," Justin said. "What's the Abominable Snowman's favorite dessert?"

Bag shrugged.

"Frozen yogurt," Justin said. "Frozen . . . Snowman . . . get it?"

Bag didn't smile. "Not meaning to offend you, my friend. But this is not laughable."

Justin sighed.

Terry came over. "Okay, guys, time to get started on lunch."

"What's on the menu today?" Justin asked.

"American chop suey," Terry said.

Justin frowned. "Never heard of it."

"What is it?" I asked.

"You know the leftover broccoli from dinner last night?" Terry said.

"Yes." We nodded.

"And the leftover spaghetti from yesterday's lunch?"

"Yes."

"And the leftover hashed brown potatoes from two days ago?"

"Yes."

"Well, we mix it all together with tomato sauce," Terry said. "Then we heat it up and sprinkle cheese on top of it. That's American chop suey."

Justin turned green. "Are you serious? It sounds more like chopped *sewage*. Just the thought of it makes me want to barf."

"Makes me want to barf, too," Terry said. "But The Blob didn't give me enough money to buy more food this week, so that's what they're gonna have to eat."

Just then Brad Schmook came into the kitchen. "I got Mr. Kirby's order for lunch. He wants a jumbo shrimp cocktail. Then a roast beef hero with peppers and onions. And a side order of potato salad. And for dessert he wants an ice-cream sundae with crushed nuts and two cherries."

"Got it," Terry said, and went to The Blob's private refrigerator.

71

Instead of leaving, Brad glanced over at Bag. "Heard you ran into a little problem last night."

Bag nodded.

Suddenly I had a funny feeling. "Hey, Brad. We think Justin and Bag were set up. We think someone told The Blob about the plan. Someone squealed."

Brad shook his head. "I wouldn't know."

After lunch, Justin and I paid Amanda a visit. A bunch of campers had tied a kid up and blindfolded him. Another camper put an apple on his head. Yet another camper stood about ten feet away with a straw.

"What are you guys doing?" Justin asked.

"We're gonna try and knock the apple off his head with spitballs," explained the kid with the straw.

"Are you crazy?" Justin said. "That'll take forever. And in the meantime you'll probably hit him in the face a million times."

"We sure hope so," the kid replied with a smile.

The line to the canteen was even longer than it had been that morning after breakfast. I saw Ralphie, the camper with the red hair and freckles. He looked a little green.

"Hey, Ralphie, what's wrong?" I asked.

"I barfed again," he groaned.

"You mean, you actually ate that American chop suey?" Justin asked.

Ralphie shook his head. "I didn't eat it. I just looked at it. Half the guys at my table hurled."

I looked up and down the line. Ralphie was right. A lot of them were holding their stomachs and looking sick.

"I guess this camp isn't so hot, huh?" Justin said.

"Actually, it's great," said one of Ralphie's friends.

"Yeah," agreed another. "No one makes you do anything. They don't care what we do."

"Tell you the truth," said Ralphie, "I love it here. It's just the food that rots."

Justin and I went up to the counter. Amanda was selling candy so fast that beads of sweat dotted her forehead.

"How are sales?" I asked.

"Incredible," Amanda said. "Everyone says lunch was the worst they've seen yet."

"What a scam," Justin said. "The campers have to eat leftovers from two days ago while The Blob gets jumbo shrimp, roast beef, and ice-cream sundaes."

"Why can't Terry take some of the money he spends on Uncle Bob's food and spend it on camp food instead?" Amanda asked.

"Because this camp isn't run for the benefit of the campers," I said. "It's run for the benefit of The Blob."

"Man, The Blob must be making a fortune," said Justin. "First he saves money by feeding the campers garbage. Then he makes money by selling them stuff at the canteen."

"Some scam, huh?" I said.

"It's totally unfair," said Amanda.

"Yeah." Justin nodded. "So why do birds fly south for the winter?"

"Uh . . ." Amanda pressed a finger against her lip. "Because it's too far to walk?"

"You are amazing." Justin shook his head in wonder. "But here's one you'll never get. What do you call an ointment that blows people up?"

Amanda scowled. "You're right. I can't imagine the answer."

"Preparation H-Bomb," Justin said with a smile.

Amanda and I groaned.

"Have you figured out who told Uncle Bob about Bag's plan to get revenge?" Amanda asked.

I looked around to make sure no one else was listening, and then spoke in a low voice. "I'm not sure, but I have a weird feeling it was Brad."

"What makes you say that?" Justin asked.

"He's the only one who knew about Bag's revenge plan *and* that we were going out for pizza the other night."

Justin's jaw dropped. "You're right! I say we get him."

"No." I shook my head. "I said it was only a feeling. I can't prove it."

Justin's shoulders sagged. "Then there's nothing we can do."

"I didn't say that," I said with a smile. Then I told them my plan.

That night just before dinner, Amanda, Justin, and I got together in the dining hall.

"Has Brad come in yet?" Justin asked.

"No," I said. "But he usually gets here with The Blob's dinner order right about now. Remember, as soon as he comes in, we start whispering. We have to make it look like we're sharing a secret."

"Here he comes," Amanda said.

We put our heads together and started to whisper. Just as I expected, Brad came toward us. "Hey, what's the big secret?"

Amanda, Justin, and I looked up like we were surprised he was there.

"Uh, nothing," I pretended to stammer. "Nothing at all."

"Oh, come on," Brad said. "You guys can trust me."

"Sorry, Brad," Justin said. "But this is a super top secret."

"And it's time for us to get back to the kitchen, anyway," I said. "Come on, Justin, let's go."

We said good-bye to Amanda and started toward the kitchen.

"You think it's gonna work?" Justin whispered as we walked away.

"Believe it," I said. "Brad will keep nagging Amanda until she finally tells him I'm planning to sneak out and get a pizza tonight."

"But how are you going to know if Brad squeals?" Justin asked.

"Because I *will* sneak out," I said. "But instead of walking down the road to the pizza place, I'll hide in the woods. If I see The Blob out there, then I'll know Brad is the rat."

Justin nodded slowly. "That's a great plan, Lucas. There's just one problem."

"What's that?" I asked.

"That means you're going into the woods tonight alone," he said.

CHAPTER

27

After dinner I stopped by the canteen and asked Amanda if Brad fell for our ruse.

"Totally." She smiled and brushed her long blond hair back. "He begged and begged me to tell him what the secret was. I kept refusing. Then finally I pretended to give in and I told him."

"Great," I said. "Now we'll see if he's the snitch."

I went back to the bunkhouse and played cards on the steps with the guys until lights-out. A couple of times I noticed Brad watching me, but I pretended that it didn't mean anything.

Finally, it was time for lights-out. I waited about ten minutes and then quietly crawled out of my bunk and slipped my clothes on.

Outside, the night air was fresh and cool. I walked down the trail to the road, but just before I got to the road, I cut off into the woods. There I hid behind a tree. If Brad was the rat, I would expect to see The Blob any second now.

I crouched behind the tree and waited. The quiet was broken now and then by the hoot of an owl. I wasn't too worried about running into Bigfoot.

Finally, I heard the faint scrape of shoes on the road. Then a clickity sound, like a dog's nails on asphalt. A few moments later I saw The Blob coming up the road with The Blob Dog on a leash.

"I expect we should be running into him pretty soon," The Blob was saying to The Blob Dog. "I'll take his pizza and let you chew on his leg. How nice of him to provide us both with a midnight snack."

That proved Brad was the snitch. I'd learned everything I needed to know. I held my breath as they went past the tree. Then I turned to go back down the trail to the camp.

Only there was someone standing in the dark behind me.

CHAPTER

28

A shiver ran down my spine. The figure just stood there in the dark. I took a sniff and knew it was Roadkill Man. The burning mix of dead-animal stench and massive body odor hung in the air between us.

"What do you want?" I asked, wiping a tear from my eye.

Roadkill Man said nothing. He didn't move. I noticed he had his stick, but not his filthy burlap bag.

"Where's your bag?" I asked.

He didn't reply.

"Hey, come on, man, loosen up," I said.

Roadkill Man raised his hand and gave me the peace sign.

I gave it back to him.

He frowned. "Why aren't you scared?"

"Why should I be scared?" I asked.

"Because I'm a hippie freak, man," he said. "I look

weird and eat dead animals I find in the road."

"Hey, it's probably better than the garbage we serve at camp," I replied. "But why *do* you eat dead animals you find on the road?"

"I love nature," he said. "Back to the land, man. Don't kill living creatures. But I have to eat. So I only eat what other people kill by accident."

"But doesn't it taste awful?" I asked.

Roadkill Man's eyes darted left and right. Then he moved closer and whispered, "To tell you the truth, man, if you cook it long enough and use enough B-2 Steak Sauce, you can make anything taste good. In fact, I'm going to cook up some gophers right now. Want to join me?"

"Uh, that's a really nice invitation," I said, thinking of Brad the Snitch. "But I have to get back to the camp. I have some unfinished business."

CHAPTER 29

"**Y**ou *talked* to Roadkill Man?" Justin gasped the next morning. We were walking from the bunkhouse to the dining hall.

A terrified-looking kid raced past. His body was covered with bread crumbs glued on with strawberry jelly. He was being chased by a bunch of laughing campers carrying stale rolls.

"Get the goose! Get the goose!" they were shouting.

"They sure play some unusual games here," Justin said, and turned back to me. "By the way, did Roadkill Man share any recipes with you?"

"Very funny, Justin." I smirked.

"Maybe we could try some on the campers," Justin said. "Like smear of deer or chunk of skunk. It couldn't be any worse than American chop suey."

We went into the dining hall. Ralphie and a crowd of his friends were waiting there for us.

"You never told me you guys worked in the kitchen," Ralphie said angrily.

"You're right," I said. "I didn't want you to know."

"How come you serve us such lousy food?" asked one of Ralphie's friends.

"We don't have a choice," Justin said. "We just cook what they give us."

"It's not fair," Ralphie complained. "You feed us crummy food we can't eat. Then we have to pay for stuff at the canteen. And we heard Mr. Kirby eats like a king."

"No one says you have to come back here next year," I said.

"I'm not worried about next year," said Ralphie. "I'm worried about the next seven weeks. At this rate I'm gonna starve to death."

Justin and I left Ralphie and his friends and headed for the canteen.

"Hey, guys," Amanda said when she saw us. "How come you look so glum?"

"We just talked to some unhappy campers," Justin said.

"They can't take the food," I added.

Amanda nodded. "I wish there was something we could do for them. In the meantime, did you find out who the snitch is?"

"It has to be Brad," I said.

Amanda narrowed her eyes angrily. "That snake! I'll never talk to him again."

"Actually, I was kind of hoping you would," I said.

"Why?" Amanda asked.

"I need to know what Brad's favorite candy is," I said.

"That's easy," said Amanda. "He loves Raisinets."

"Perfect," I said with a smile. "Listen, I'll need two Hershey's bars and a box of Raisinets. And if you see Brad, do me a favor and be really nice."

"If you say so," Amanda replied. "But it won't be easy."

Justin and I went into the kitchen.

"So what's the story?" Justin asked.

"I need a pair of long tweezers," I said. "And a razor blade and some clear glue. You can get the glue from arts and crafts. Try the nurse for the razor and tweezers."

Justin made a face. "I don't get it."

"You will," I said.

Justin got the tweezers and the glue. We began work during the break between breakfast and lunch. Terry was on the phone with Doris as usual.

"Of course I love you, sweetheart," he was saying. "Yes, I promise I'll be there as soon as I know dinner is done tonight. . . . What? You want me to come over *now*? But I can't, honey. I have to get lunch started in half an hour. . . . Yes, I do love you! Okay, okay, I'll come now, but I won't be able to stay long."

He hung up the receiver and turned to Justin and me. "Listen, I gotta go for a little while. You guys have to take care of lunch. I'll be back as soon as I can."

Terry left the kitchen.

I handed Justin the two Hershey's bars. "Melt these down until they're like mud."

"I still don't get it," Justin said as he unwrapped the candy bars and placed them in a small pan. While he did that, I used the razor blade to carefully undo the cellophane around the box of Raisinets. Then I carefully opened the box itself. I poured about half the Raisinets out and shared them with Justin, Bag, and the orphan Sherpas.

"How are those Hershey's bars doing?" I asked Justin.

"Just about melted," Justin replied.

"Great." I went to the refrigerator and got out Terry's jar of cold flies.

"Oh, wow." Justin grinned. "*Now* I get it!"

CHAPTER

30

The flies were too cold to move. Using the tweezers, we dipped about two dozen of the biggest, plumpest flies into the melted chocolate. We quickly put them on a plate back in the refrigerator so that the chocolate would harden and the flies wouldn't get too lively.

"Chocolate-covered flies," Justin said. "This is almost as good as what Roadkill Man must eat. By the way, I came up with some new recipes. What do you think of poodles with noodles?"

"Gross," I said.

"So did you hear about the woman who was on a ship and fell overboard?" Justin asked.

"No," I said.

"A huge shark swam up to her," Justin said. "It was just about to take a bite, but then it swam away."

"Why?" I asked.

"Because it was a *man*-eating shark," he said. "Man-eating, not woman-eating, get it?"

"Yuck, yuck." I groaned.

When the chocolate around the flies was hard, we mixed them in with the Raisinets and put them back in the box. Using the glue, I sealed the box and the cellophane around it. Then I put the whole box in the refrigerator.

"Step one of Operation Chocolate Fly is now complete," I announced.

Step two of Operation Chocolate Fly began after lunch. Terry came back from seeing Doris. Justin and I took the box of Raisinets out of the refrigerator and paid Amanda a visit.

"Here's a special box of Raisinets," I said, handing the box to her. "Keep it in a cool place and then sell it to Brad."

"With pleasure," Amanda said.

Justin and I had to go back to the kitchen to start dinner. We left an orphan Sherpa out in the dining hall, wiping down the tables with a towel. His job was to let us know as soon as Brad arrived at the canteen.

About an hour later, the orphan Sherpa hurried into the kitchen and whispered something to Bag. Bag gave me the nod.

"Hey, Terry," I said. "Think Justin and I could take a short break?"

"Go ahead," Terry said.

Justin and I left the kitchen. Brad was already at the canteen, leaning on the counter, talking to Amanda.

Justin and I sat down at a table. We were too far away to hear what Brad said to Amanda, but it sounded like he was again trying to get her to take a walk in the woods.

Amanda kept on politely refusing. Finally Brad gave up. "Okay, let me have a box of Raisinets," he said.

Amanda sold him a box. Brad opened it and started to walk toward us.

"Hey, guys, how's it going?" He acted friendly as usual.

"Okay, Brad," Justin said. "How about you?"

"Same as always." Brad brought the box of Raisinets to his lips. Then he tilted his head back and let a bunch slide into his mouth. He started to chew them.

"You hear anything about someone going out for pizza last night?" Brad asked. He was still chewing.

"Not me," I said.

"Not me, either," said Justin.

Brad swallowed. Then he placed the box of Raisinets against his lips and poured in another mouthful. He chewed them for a while, then stopped and made a face.

"These taste kind of stale," he said.

Then he swallowed the *second* mouthful.

"Hey, Brad," I said, holding out my hand. "Can I see that box?"

Brad eyed me suspiciously. "You're not going to take any, are you?"

"Oh, no," I said. "I wouldn't dream of it. In fact, instead of giving me the box, why don't you just pour a couple of Raisinets out here on the table."

I pointed at a spot on the table where the sunlight came through the window.

"Why?" Brad asked.

"I just want to see something," I said.

Brad frowned, but he poured out a couple of Raisinets on the table. They laid motionless in the sunlight.

Brad took another mouthful of Raisinets. "What's the point?" he asked as he chewed. "They're just gonna melt."

"That's not all they're going to do," said Justin.

"Huh?" Brad stared down at the Raisinets. The little candies began to glisten as the chocolate started to melt in the sunlight.

Then one of the Raisinets moved.

"What the . . . ?" Brad swallowed his third mouthful of Raisinets.

A tiny black leg poked through the melting chocolate and wiggled.

"I don't believe it!" Brad gasped.

As he watched in amazement, more tiny black legs

worked their way through the chocolate. Finally, the chocolate-covered fly managed to turn upright and began to stagger across the tabletop, leaving a thin trail of melted chocolate behind it.

"A chocolate-covered fly!" Brad said. "I wonder how *that* got in my box?"

I winked at Justin.

"Good thing I didn't eat that one," Brad said, and turned toward a garbage can.

"Hey, what are you doing?" I asked.

"Throwing the box away," Brad said. "I'm not eating anything that had a chocolate-covered fly in it."

"Don't throw it out," I said. "Pour the rest out on the table."

Brad frowned and poured out the rest of the Raisinets. As they lay in the sun, about half of them began to wriggle and sprout tiny legs.

"Kind of like watching little chocolate eggs hatch," Justin commented.

Brad's eyes widened as he watched the chocolate-covered flies come alive.

"Gee," he gasped. "At least half of them are flies."

"Know what that means?" I asked. "At least half the ones you *ate* were flies, too."

Brad's jaw dropped. He stared at us in shock.

"That'll teach you to be a snitch," Justin said.

I'm not sure Brad heard us. He had his hands over his mouth and was running toward the bathroom.

CHAPTER 31

Everyone in the kitchen was in a good mood that night. Bag gave Justin and me high fives.

"To you I am giving thanks, my friends," he said. "I am being glad that you have performed this revenge on Brad. This guy is being very much deserving it for squealing on us."

"I bet that's the last time he snitches on anyone," Justin said.

Only Terry looked annoyed. "Who said you could use my flies?"

"Oh, come on, man, give us a break," I said. "I'll replace them if you really want."

"Darn right you will," Terry said, handing me his butterfly net.

Later, Justin, Bag, and I finished making dinner. Terry was on the phone with Doris again. "Aw, come on, honey, *you know* I love you. Yes, I'll be there tonight. I *promise.*"

We cleaned up the kitchen and decided to take a swim in the lake. We were about to leave when The Blob appeared. His face was red, and he looked mad. "How many times have I told you to stay off that phone?" he growled at Terry.

Terry quickly hung up the receiver. The Blob turned to Justin and me. "Where do you think you're going?"

"Uh, to take a swim in the lake," Justin said.

"You're both confined to the bunkhouse," The Blob said. "For the next week you'll stay in the bunkhouse except when you're working."

"Why?" I asked.

"You know why," The Blob growled. "And next Friday night plan to work late. I'm having a golf outing and a cookout for my friends."

"But next Friday is our day off," Justin said. "You already took away our last day off."

"Well, I'm taking your next day off, too," The Blob grumbled. Then he turned and left the kitchen.

CHAPTER

Back in the bunkhouse I started to pack. This time no one was going to stop me. I was out of there.

"Lucas, you can't go," Justin said. Bag and the others were there. Terry was visiting Doris as usual. Brad was in the infirmary after barfing up chocolate-covered flies all day. He wouldn't be able to tell The Blob I was leaving.

"Forget it, man," I said. "Don't even try to stop me."

"We are needing you in the fight against this Blob," Bag said.

"I'm sorry, Bag, but that's not my fight," I said.

Bag's shoulders sagged, and he turned away. Justin moved close and started to whisper about Amanda, but I still shook my head.

"Sorry," I said. "If you want to come with me, fine. If you want to stay, that's your business."

Nothing they said could stop me. I pulled my

backpack over my shoulder and headed out.

"Lucas, wait!" a voice called. I turned and saw Amanda coming toward me in the dark. Justin must've told her I was leaving. I stopped, and she came up to me. "Please don't go," she said.

That was strange. "Why do you care?" I asked.

Amanda gazed down at the ground. I guess she was embarrassed. "I do care, Lucas. I wish you wouldn't go. Who's going to protect the orphan Sherpas and Ralphie and the other kids? Who's going to get back at Uncle Bob for all the awful things he's done?"

"I'm sorry, Amanda," I said. "I just can't take this abuse anymore."

"Did you hear that Uncle Bob is having a golf outing and a cookout next week for his friends?" Amanda asked. "Think of all the food he's going to order for it. Wouldn't it be great if we could give that food to the campers instead?"

"Dream on, Amanda," I said.

Amanda hung her head and nodded. "I just wish there was something we could do. I thought if anyone could do it, it would be you."

I headed down the trail out of camp in the dark. I figured I could sleep in the woods behind Log Cabin Pizza that night, then wait for the bus the next day. I felt bad about leaving Justin and Amanda and Bag and the others. Amanda's words rang in my ears.

95

Maybe she was right. Maybe I was letting the rest of the camp down. But I'd made up my mind. I was out of there.

Then a voice behind me said, "Slow down, man. Where are you going?"

CHAPTER

33

I stopped and stood still in the dark. A shiver ran down my spine. I turned around slowly, expecting to find The Blob and The Blob Dog behind me. But the figure who came out of the shadows was scrawny and bearded. He was carrying a stick and a bag over his shoulder.

It was Roadkill Man. He held up his hand and gave me the peace sign.

I breathed a sigh of relief. Then the odor hit and my eyes started to water.

"Where are you off to?" he asked.

"I'm leaving," I said. "This time for good."

"Can't say I blame you, man," he said with a nod. "But you won't get far tonight. Where were you planning to stay?"

I told him I planned to sleep in the woods behind Log Cabin Pizza.

"I wouldn't do that," Roadkill Man said. "The bears

go through the garbage at night. They don't take kindly to strangers. Why don't you crash at my place tonight?"

Given a choice between staying with Roadkill Man or the bears, the answer was pretty obvious.

Roadkill Man led me through the forest in the dark. The stench was pretty bad, but after a while my nose must've gotten numbed by it. Soon we came to the hill where the forest-rangers' tower stood. He started to climb the hill and I followed. About halfway up, Roadkill Man stopped near a large, flat rock. He pushed the rock sideways, and it rolled like a big stone wheel.

Behind it was a dark cavern.

"You live in a cave?" I asked.

"Back to the land, man," Roadkill Man said, stepping inside.

I peered into the darkness. "How do you see?"

"Oh, almost forgot." Roadkill Man reached toward the wall and flicked a switch. Suddenly the cave was ablaze with light. I couldn't believe it!

"You have a cave with electric light?" I asked in amazement.

"For sure, man," said Roadkill Man. "I've got satellite TV and Internet Access, too. Want a Coke?"

We settled down in Roadkill Man's living room. The furniture was all old junk he'd found along the side of the road — milk crates, wooden wire spools, cinder blocks. An old wooden golf club leaned in a corner. But in the center of the room was a huge Sony TV with remote everything. And along the wall was an awesome-looking sound system with a tape player, CD, and turntable.

"What do you want to watch?" he asked, clicking the remote and turning on the TV. "I got all the sports and movie channels. Home Shopping Network, too."

"You get MTV?" I asked.

"Right on, man. MTV, M2, VH-1, country, you name it." Roadkill Man handed me a cold Coke. "Sit back and relax, man. Take a load off. Float downstream. I'll be in the kitchen. I've got a mess of gopher I've got to skin and clean."

CHAPTER 34

I watched MTV for a while, but something was bothering me. Finally, I went into the kitchen. Except for the rocky walls, it looked like any other kitchen, with a stove, refrigerator, kitchen counter, and sink. I noticed several cases of B-2 Steak Sauce stacked in a corner.

Roadkill Man was standing at the sink, humming to himself as he sliced up gophers. A couple of gopher skins were lying on the counter. On the floor next to him was a plastic pail full of brown, green, and purple gopher guts.

"What do you do with that stuff?" I asked.

"The intestines and internal organs?" Roadkill Man said. "Return it to the earth, man. I can't eat it, but it makes great earthworm chow."

"There's something I don't understand," I said. "I thought you lived in the woods because you were too poor to live anywhere else. But if you can afford TV and a satellite dish, you must have some money."

"Some, but not much," said Roadkill Man. "Just enough to afford the important things in life — TV, good tunes, computer games."

"But you could eat at Log Cabin Pizza," I said.

"Too many carbohydrates, man." Roadkill Man shook his head. "Besides, tomato sauce gives me the farts. Stick with proteins. That's nature's way."

"But couldn't you buy meat in a store instead of scraping it off the road?" I asked.

"Listen, man, this is lean, natural meat," he said, lifting a skinned gopher up by the tail. It was all red and bloody and still had its head and claws. "And it's *fresh*. Not like that stuff in the stores. I don't have to worry about all those growth hormones and pesticides you get in beef and chicken, either. I'd rather starve than eat the chemicals they put in those things."

On the side of the kitchen counter was an iron thing with a crank attached. Roadkill Man put the raw meat from the gopher in it and turned the crank. Out of a spout came red meat that looked a lot like hamburger.

"What's that?" I asked.

"A meat grinder," Roadkill Man said. "Can't make a good gopherburger without it."

I went back into the living room and watched TV. Soon I heard a sizzling sound and smelled the scent of cooking meat. Roadkill Man joined me in front of the TV. He put his plate on a small folding table, and sprinkled steak sauce on a gopherburger.

"Want one?" he asked.

"Uh, no thanks," I said. "I had a big meal before I left camp."

Roadkill Man took a bite of the gopherburger. "So you decided to split," he said. "Take the nonviolent approach. Right on, man. Peace and love. Flower power. You can't fight the Bob Kirbys of this world. If you try, they'll crush you. Go back to the land. Live in a cave. Peace, brother."

Suddenly I felt bad that I was running away. That I'd left my friends. It wasn't right. I had to stay and fight. The Blob may have seemed unbeatable, but he had to have a weakness.

Later that night I stepped quietly into the bunk-house. It was dark, and the orphan Sherpas were sleeping soundly. I went over to my bunk and started to get undressed.

"Huh, who's that?" Justin asked groggily.

"Me, Lucas," I whispered.

Justin sat up in bed with his eyes wide. "You're back!?"

"Keep it down," I whispered. "You'll wake everyone."

"Why'd you come back?" Justin whispered.

"I didn't want to miss The Blob's big cookout," I whispered.

The next week I snuck out of camp each afternoon while The Blob played golf. I'd arrive at Roadkill Man's cave with an empty plastic pail, and leave with a full one. Full of gopher, squirrel, raccoon, and deer guts.

Justin, Bag, and I hid the pails of animal guts in the back of one of the industrial-size refrigerators.

"I don't get it," Justin whispered one night while we cooked dinner for the campers. "What are you gonna do with all those guts?"

"You'll see," I said.

"If you are thinking to feed these guts to this Blob, you are being mistaken," Bag said. "This Blob is believing he is the eater of fine foods. He is not eating these greenish guts."

I smiled. "Just wait, Bag."

* * *

The day before The Blob's big cookout, a truck pulled up behind the camp kitchen. The Blob came into the kitchen. Terry was on the phone to Doris, as usual.

"For the last time, get off that darn phone!" The Blob yelled at him. "Tell everyone to stop what they're doing and help unload the truck."

We all went to the truck and started to unload it.

Justin and I carried in boxes of top-quality ground beef for hamburgers. The orphan Sherpas brought in cans of baked beans and bags of potatoes for potato salad. Bag brought in hundreds of hamburger rolls.

"Doesn't it just kill you?" Justin whispered to me. "This is what the campers should be eating, not The Blob's friends."

"Yes." I nodded. "It sure does kill me. But not for long."

CHAPTER 36

The next day was The Blob's big cookout. Right after lunch, Terry told us to start preparing for it.

"We have to take all that ground beef and turn it into hamburger patties," he announced. "We have to peel all these potatoes and boil them for potato salad. And we have to cook all these beans. So get to work."

"What about dinner for the campers?" Justin asked.

"Looks like they're getting American chop suey again," Terry said. "Bag, check the refrigerators and see what leftovers we have. Justin and Lucas, start peeling potatoes."

Just then The Blob came in and started telling Terry how he wanted the food prepared for the party. He had just finished when Bag spoke up. "I am sorry to be reporting that we are not having enough food for the campers for tonight," he said. "Even if we are mixing all the leftovers into American chop suey."

The Blob rubbed his double chin and looked around the kitchen. His eyes stopped at Justin and me. We were busy peeling potatoes.

"Use the potato peels," The Blob said.

"Excuse me, sir?" Terry replied.

"I said, use the potato peels," The Blob repeated. "Grind them up and add them to the American chop suey. That'll fill out the meal."

"Potato peels?" Terry looked ill.

"It just so happens that the skin is the most nutritious part of the potato," The Blob said. "So, *use it!*"

Then he turned and stormed out of the kitchen.

Terry turned to the rest of us. "You heard him. Grind up those potato peels and add them to the American chop suey."

We did as we were told.

"What do you call a camel that has to go to the bathroom?" Justin asked.

"I can't imagine," I said.

"Humpty Dumpty," said Justin. "What do you give a seasick elephant?"

I shook my head.

"Lots of room," said Justin.

I just rolled my eyes.

It took a couple of hours to peel all the potatoes, but we finally finished the job. Terry looked at his watch. "Okay, guys, now it's time to make hamburgers."

That meant it was time for us to start Operation Gopher Gutburger. Justin and I gave each other a look.

"Hey, Terry," I said. "Can't I get a break? I've been working nonstop since six this morning."

"Okay," Terry said. "Five minutes."

That was all the time I needed.

I left the kitchen and went out into the dining hall. As usual, the line to the canteen went on forever.

"Hey, Lucas!" someone called.

I stopped and looked. It was Ralphie.

"Hey, how are you doing?" I asked.

"Lousy," Ralphie complained. "I'm starving. I've lost five pounds since camp started. Look at me. I'm skin and bones."

He was right. He looked skinny, and his clothes hardly fit him.

"Can't you guys serve us something good for dinner tonight?" Ralphie begged. "*Please!* Another lousy meal and I'm gonna start eating the bark off the trees."

"You may be in luck," I said.

Ralphie's jaw dropped. "You *serious*?"

"I'll do my best," I said, then went down the line

to the canteen counter. Amanda was behind the counter, selling candy as fast as she could.

"The plan's in motion," I said in a low voice.

"Okay," Amanda replied. "Give me a minute."

Back in the kitchen, I started to help Justin make hamburger patties from the big packages of ground beef that had been delivered the previous day.

A few moments later the phone rang. Terry answered it. "Hello? Oh, hey, baby...what? Right now? But I can't. I'm in the middle of preparing the fat man's big cookout. Of course, I...hey, wait a minute! Who is this? You don't sound like Doris."

Justin and I shared a panicked look.

We watched Terry's face as he held the phone to his ear.

He was frowning.

What if he didn't believe it was Doris?

We were sunk!

But then Terry's expression changed. "You have a sore throat? No wonder your voice sounds so different. Okay, okay, baby, I'll be right there."

He hung up and turned to the rest of us. "Listen, guys, I have to go somewhere. Keep making those hamburger patties. I'll be back as soon as I can."

Terry left the kitchen.

Justin and I exchanged high fives. Operation Gopher Gutburger was right on schedule!

Bag and Justin got the pails of animal guts from the refrigerator while I set up the industrial-size food processor.

"Here's the deal, guys," I said. "We're going to make two sets of hamburgers. The orphan Sherpas will make real hamburgers. We'll serve those to the campers. In the meantime, Bag, Justin, and I are going to make gopher gutburgers. Those will be for The Blob's cookout."

"Please be excusing me, my friend," Bag said. "But how are we making these gopher gutburgers?"

"We'll mix equal parts of hamburger and gopher guts," I said, then took a pound of hamburger and four big greenish gobs of guts and put it all into the food processor. Then I mixed it.

"What do you think, guys?" I asked a little later as we inspected the results.

"Well, it definitely looks reddish, like hamburger," Justin said.

"But it is being sort of loose and of a watery nature," added Bag. "I am thinking we are needing to mix something starchy into this to be making it firmer."

Justin and I shared a questioning look. Then, at the same moment, we both gasped, "Potato peels!"

It wasn't long before the orphan Sherpas were making the real hamburger patties while we prepared patties made of hamburger, ground-up animal guts, and potato peels. As the kitchen grew hotter, it began to fill with a foul odor.

"I hate to say this," Justin said, as we kept making the gopher gutburger patties. "These things may *look* like hamburgers, but they sure don't *smell* like hamburgers."

"That's because we haven't added the magic ingredient," I said.

"What magic ingredient?" a voice asked.

CHAPTER

39

Brad Schmook was standing at the kitchen door.

"Oh, hi, Brad," I said nervously. "We haven't seen much of you lately. What brings you here?"

"Cut the friendly act, Lucas," Brad grumbled. "You know why I'm here. Mr. Kirby sent me to make sure you guys were getting ready for his cookout tonight."

He started toward us. With our feet, Justin and I shoved the pails of animal guts under the stainless-steel counters. But the closer Brad came, the more chance there was that he'd notice something was strange.

"Hey, Brad," Justin said. "Want some Raisinets?"

"Get lost, Justin," Brad muttered angrily. "Ever since you slipped me those chocolate-covered flies I can't even *look* at a Raisinet without feeling ill."

Meanwhile, he was coming closer. "You guys are supposed to be making potato salad. Where is it?"

"Over here." I showed him all the potatoes we'd boiled.

"Okay, now how about the hamburgers?" Brad asked.

"We're working on them right now," I said.

"Where?" Brad asked.

"Uh . . ." I didn't know what to say. If I showed Brad a gopher gutburger, there was a chance he'd figure out what was going on.

Just then Brad wrinkled his nose. "Hey, what's that smell?"

"Uh . . . some milk went bad," I quickly said.

Brad narrowed his eyes at me. "You *sure*?"

"Totally," I said.

"And what about those hamburgers?" Brad asked.

Suddenly I had an idea. "Maybe you'd like to try one?"

40

Brad thought for a moment, then nodded. "Good idea. I'd love a nice juicy hamburger. I'm sick of the garbage you guys serve."

I grabbed a burger and threw it on the grill. Justin waved his hand, trying to get my attention. But I had to ignore him because Brad had begun sniffing around again.

"You sure that smell is sour milk?" he asked. "It smells more like spoiled meat to me."

Everyone was giving everyone else nervous looks. Justin was making all kinds of faces at me.

"Spoiled meat!? That's ridiculous!" I forced a laugh, then quickly turned to Bag. "Hey, Bag, take Brad over to the refrigerator and show him the fresh chopped meat we're using."

"This I am being glad to do right away." Bag took Brad to the refrigerator. Meanwhile, Justin nudged me with his elbow.

"What are you doing?" he whispered.

"I'm giving Brad a hamburger," I whispered back. "That way, he'll think we're going to cook the good burgers at The Blob's cookout."

"There's just one problem," Justin whispered. "You're not cooking a *real* hamburger. You're cooking a *gopher gutburger*!"

I spun around and looked at the grill. Justin was right! In my haste to distract Brad, I'd picked up a gopher gutburger by mistake!

"If Brad tastes that thing, he's going to know something's wrong!" Justin hissed.

The situation looked bad . . . until I remembered the *magic* ingredient.

I reached under the counter and came up with a bottle of B-2 Steak Sauce. While Bag showed Brad the good hamburger in the refrigerator, I poured the sauce over the gopher gutburger.

Brad came back from the refrigerator. "That meat looks okay." He stopped and smiled. "Hey, what's *that* smell? That smells *great*!"

I flipped the gopher gutburger onto a hamburger roll and handed it to him. "That is a fresh, delicious, juicy hamburger."

Brad opened his mouth and was just about to take a bite when he stopped.

Around the room, everyone held their breath. Was something wrong?

"Got any ketchup?" Brad asked.

"Coming right up." Justin tossed him a couple of ketchup packets.

Brad tore one open and squeezed the ketchup out. Then he took a big bite of the gopher gutburger.

Everyone waited.

Brad chewed.

The kitchen was so quiet, you could have heard a mouse burp.

Brad swallowed.

For a moment he didn't say a thing.

Then he nodded. "I hate to admit it, guys, but this is one tasty burger."

Brad left to report back to The Blob that good food was being prepared for the cookout. As soon as he left, the kitchen went berserk.

"He is being in love with it!" Bag cried.

"Do you believe it!?" Justin gasped. "He ate a burger that was mostly gopher guts and potato peels and he thought it was great!"

Justin started to do a little dance and sing:

"Great green gobs of greasy grimy gopher guts
Mutilated monkey meat
Chopped-up birdy's feet
French-fried eyeballs rolling up and down the
    street
Oops! I forgot my spoon!

The Blob's gonna eat gutburgers!
The Blob's gonna eat gutburgers!
Snort some pork, he's such a dork!
The Blob's gonna eat gutburgers!"

Justin didn't notice that the rest of us had stopped celebrating.

Finally I nudged him with my elbow. "Uh, Justin?"

Justin stopped dancing. "What?"

I nodded toward the kitchen door.

Terry was standing there with his hand on his hips. And he didn't look happy.

CHAPTER

41

Terry started to walk through the kitchen.

No one said a word.

"Gopher gutburgers?" he said.

"Well, not — " I started to say.

Terry held up his hand. "Shut up, Lucas. I heard the whole thing. You're not gonna talk your way out of this one."

He stopped by the counter, picked up one of the gut buckets, and sniffed it. "Gross!" He hurled the bucket away. "I can't believe you guys thought you could get away with this. I can't believe you thought you could trick me into thinking that was Doris on the phone."

Terry walked over to the rows of gopher gutburger patties that Bag, Justin, and I had made. He bent down and sniffed one.

"Blech!" he gasped. "You really planned to feed this to The Blob?"

"We just gave one to Brad, and he loved it," I said.

118

Bag and Justin smiled at the memory of Brad savoring that disgusting burger.

"Wipe those smiles off your faces!" Terry shouted. He picked up the bottle of B-2 Steak Sauce. "This stuff must be pretty good to mask the flavor of gopher guts and potato peels, huh?"

No one answered.

Terry glared at us. "You know what I ought to do? I ought to make you guys eat each and every one of these gopher gutburgers. I ought to make you eat them *raw*."

Bag winced. Justin looked a little green. Just the thought of eating a raw gopher gutburger was enough to make you sick. I couldn't think of anything more disgusting.

Terry continued to glare at us. "Yeah," he said. "That's what I should do. Make you eat every one of them raw."

No one said a word.

Very slowly, Terry's glare became a grin. "But I'm not going to do that. Instead, I'm going to let you serve them to The Blob and his friends."

Justin, Bag, and I traded astonished looks. "But why?" I asked.

"Why?" Terry raised his eyebrows. "I'll tell you why. Because I'm sick of that big fat tub of lard bossing everyone around. I'm sick of him eating good food while those poor campers out there eat garbage. But most of all, I'm sick of him making it so hard for me to talk to my darling Doris."

CHAPTER

42

That evening Justin and I went to The Blob's big yellow and white house to prepare for the cookout. Meanwhile, back in the camp kitchen, Terry and Bag cooked the good hamburgers, and the orphan Sherpas served them to the campers.

In The Blob's backyard, Justin and I grilled up plenty of gopher gutburgers with B-2 Steak Sauce for The Blob and his friends.

"This is a great burger, Bob!" A tall, blond-haired man patted The Blob on the back. "My compliments to the chef."

"Thank you." The Blob beamed with pride. Meanwhile The Blob Dog sat in his pen, drooling.

"Uh, excuse me, Mr. Kirby," Justin said. "Do you think your dog might like a burger?"

"Of course," The Blob replied. "Excellent idea. Only he likes his meat raw."

"No problem." Justin winked at me and took a nice

juicy raw gopher gutburger over to the pen. "Here you go, pooch." He tossed the burger over the fence, and The Blob Dog gobbled it up hungrily.

Everyone came back for seconds on the gopher gutburgers. The Blob even had thirds!

"These are the best burgers I've ever tasted, boys," he said happily. "In fact, I'm going to make sure you work at my next cookout as well!"

After Justin and I finished cooking the gutburgers for The Blob, we went back to the dining hall. The campers were just finishing their dinners. When they saw us, the whole camp stood up and applauded. Amanda came up to us.

"How do they know?" Justin asked.

"They don't," Amanda said. "All they know is that they're eating good food for once! How did the cookout go?"

I had to smile. "The Blob loved his gopher gutburgers."

"Then, you did it!" Amanda cried happily, and threw her arms around my neck and kissed me on the cheek.

"Hey, what about me?" Justin pouted.

"You, too!" Amanda put her arms around his neck and kissed him.

When she let go, Justin had a goofy look on his face, and his eyes were rolling around loosely in his head.

Then Ralphie came up. "Thanks, guys. This was the best meal I've had since I got here." Then he put his hand over his mouth and started to look a little green. "Oops! I think I'm going to barf."

"Why?" I asked.

"I can't help it," Ralphie said. "I'm just not used to good food!"

Ralphie ran toward the bathroom. The rest of us smiled.

"You know," Justin said, "that reminds me of a joke. Did you hear about the guy in the restaurant who told the waiter his soup tasted funny?"

"Let me guess," said Amanda. "The waiter said, 'If your soup tastes funny, why aren't you laughing?' "

Justin got that goofy look on his face again. "I think I'm in love!"